"Who Invented Brothers, Anyway?"

Greg Evans

TOR®

A TOM DOHERTY ASSOCIATES BOOK
NEW YORK

LUANN: "WHO INVENTED BROTHERS, ANYWAY?"

Copyright © 1986, 1989 by King Feature Syndicate, Inc.

A Tor Book
Published by Tom Doherty Associates, Inc.
49 West 24 Street
New York, N.Y. 10010

ISBN: 0-812-57225-4   Can. ISBN: 0-812-57226-2

First edition: June 1989

Printed in the United States of America

0 9 8 7 6 5 4 3 2 1

2-3

I CAN'T BELIEVE MR. FOGARTY PUT AARON HILL IN THE DESK RIGHT BEHIND ME!!

ALL OF A SUDDEN, ENGLISH IS MY FAVORITE SUBJECT!

"TO TIFFANY"

A Valentine Poem to A.H.

OH, AARON HILL, I THINK I SHOULD
(IN FACT I KNOW I *MUST*)
BOLDLY TELL YOU OF MY LOVE...

FROM: ANONYMOUS

2-14

I KEEP HOPING AARON HILL WILL GIVE ME A VALENTINE CARD, DELTA

LUANN, AARON IS ONE OF THE CUTEST GUYS IN THE WHOLE SCHOOL. MAYBE YOU'D BE BETTER OFF IF YOU LIKED SOMEONE WHO'S MORE LIKE YOU

2·15

WHY WOULD I WANT TO LIKE SOMEONE WHO'S LIKE ME?

GREG

BERNICE, DID YOU EVER NOTICE THAT FRECKLE ON TIFFANY'S EAR LOBE?

SHE'S ALSO GOT A LITTLE BIRTHMARK ON HER ANKLE

AND SHE THINKS SHE'S *SO* PERFECT

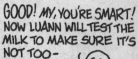

© News America Syndicate, 1986

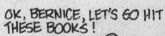

3·16

PUDDLES! CAN'T YOU SLEEP SOMEPLACE THAT'S NOT IN MY WAY?!

greg 3-23

CLASS, I WANT YOU TO WRITE ABOUT 20 THINGS YOU DID OVER EASTER VACATION

4.1

"Twenty Things I did over Easter Vacation." By Luann DeGroot
I went to the mall

twenty times

GREG

I'VE GOT A BOOK REPORT DUE FRIDAY, A MATH TEST TOMORROW, AN OVERDUE SCIENCE PROJECT AND FOUR HOURS OF HOMEWORK!

WONDER IF THEY'D LET ME BACK INTO THE THIRD GRADE?

greg

4·3

BRAD DeGROOT, I AM NEVER, EVER GOING TO SPEAK TO YOU AGAIN !!!

WELL, WHATEVER I DID I WISH I'D DONE IT YEARS AGO !!

HOW CAN I GET A's AND B's IN SUBJECTS THAT GIVE ME Z's?

4-22

GREG

THERE!!

WHERE?

I FINALLY GOT MY SCHOOL ROUTE ALL WORKED OUT, BERNICE!

SCHOOL ROUTE?

YEAH. I ARRIVE AT SCHOOL THROUGH HALL 'C' SO I CAN STOP IN THE RESTROOM AND FIX MY HAIR

THEN I CIRCLE AROUND TO BUILDING 'D' SO I CAN SEE AARON HILL AT HIS LOCKER

AFTER P.E., I NEED TO RE-FIX MY HAIR SO I HEAD BACK TO HALL 'C'. THEN I RUN ACROSS THE LAWN TO BUILDING 'A' IN TIME TO SEE AARON ENTER SOCIAL STUDIES

© News America Syndicate, 1986

AT NOON, I CUT THROUGH THE GYM SO I CAN SIT NEAR AARON'S TABLE IN THE CAFETERIA

© News America Syndicate, 1986

SEEMS LIKE 12TH GRADE WILL NEVER GET HERE

WHAT ARE YOU
TALKING ABOUT,
LUANN?

A Poem by Luann DeGroot

"Unnecessary Stuff"

TO THOSE WHO MAKE UP SCHOOL DESIGNS:
STUDENTS DON'T NEED EXIT SIGNS!

... SO I SAY, "BUT MOM, *EVERYONE'S* GOING!"

AND SHE SAYS, "LUANN, I'M NOT EVERYONE'S MOTHER. I'M *YOUR* MOTHER AND I SAY YOU'RE NOT GOING!"

I WONDER IF HASSLES LIKE THIS HAPPEN IN OTHER FAMILIES?